USBORNE DOLL'S HOUSE STICKER BOOK

COUNTRY HOUSE GARDEN

Illustrated by Lucy Grossmith
Designed by Lucy Wain
Written by Struan Reid

Contents

You'll find the sticker pages at the back of the book.

SAFFRON MANOR
GARDEN MAP

This brick manor house set in the countryside
was built more than 300 years ago.
Over the centuries, different kinds of gardens
were laid out around the house, reflecting the
tastes and interests of successive owners.

CONSERVATORY

PERGOLA GARDEN

WILD FLOWER GARDEN

HERBACEOUS BORDER

MAZE

Oak, beech, lime and
chestnut trees are dotted
around the park.

An ancient deer park surrounds the manor and its gardens.

THE MANOR

SUNKEN GARDEN

TERRACE GARDEN

FORMAL GARDEN

FOUNTAIN GARDEN

GARDEN OF DISCOVERY

ORANGERY

WALLED GARDEN

ORCHARD

Crinkle crankle wall

3

FORMAL GARDEN

TERRACE GARDEN

8

SUNKEN GARDEN

9

FOUNTAIN GARDEN

ORANGERY

Place this sun parasol over the white table.

This white bench can go near the bicycle.

The plants in pots can be dotted along the stone terrace.

Sun lounger

Cushions make it more comfortable sitting on the grass.

Lantern

Sun hat

These picnic baskets can go next to the rug on the grass.

Cut flowers

Someone has been reading this book on the grass.

Butter

Plates of food and glasses of lemonade for the picnic

Potted plant

Newspaper

Tea pot

Prop this bicycle against the stone balustrade.

Cut flowers

Parasol

PERGOLA GARDEN

HERBACEOUS BORDER

GARDEN OF
DISCOVERY

CONSERVATORY

USBORNE QUICKLINKS

For links to websites where you can take virtual tours of real
country house gardens and find out more about some of the plants
grown in them, go to the Usborne Quicklinks website at
www.usborne.com/quicklinks
and enter the keywords 'Country House Garden'.
Please follow the internet safety guidelines at the
Usborne Quicklinks website.

Edited by Jane Chisholm. Managing designer: Nicola Butler. Digital manipulation by John Russell.
First published in 2017 by Usborne Publishing Ltd., Usborne House, 83-85 Saffron Hill, London EC1N 8RT, England. www.usborne.com

FORMAL GARDEN
(PAGES 4-5)

These evergreen trees have been clipped into different shapes. Place them in the flowerbeds.

Put these marble statues on the grass circles.

These small clipped trees can go at the bottom of the steps.

These wooden benches can sit against the hedge, on either side of the steps.

Gardener's gloves

TERRACE GARDEN
(PAGES 6-7)

Pot plant

Arrange these chairs and table on the stone terrace.

SUNKEN GARDEN
(PAGES 8-9)

Place the heavy stone benches next to the pond.

Water spout for the small pool on the back wall

This cat is watching the fish in the pond.

Place this water tank against the back wall.

These flower pots can go around the edge of the pond.

Daisy the dachshund

This small clipped tree can go on top of the wall.

FOUNTAIN GARDEN
(PAGES 10-11)

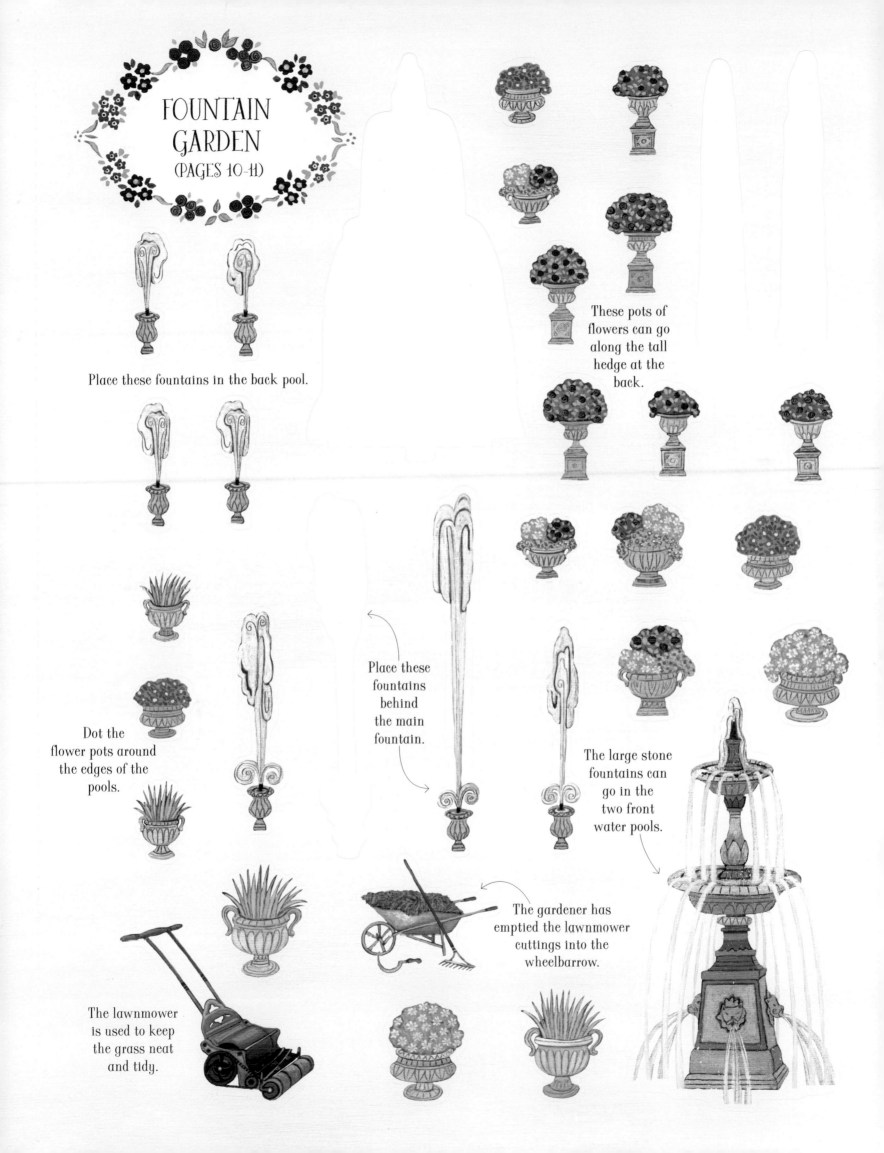

Place these fountains in the back pool.

These pots of flowers can go along the tall hedge at the back.

Dot the flower pots around the edges of the pools.

Place these fountains behind the main fountain.

The large stone fountains can go in the two front water pools.

The gardener has emptied the lawnmower cuttings into the wheelbarrow.

The lawnmower is used to keep the grass neat and tidy.

ORANGERY
(PAGES 12-13)

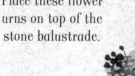

Prop this parasol against a chair.

Lemon tree

In summer, the gardeners put the orange and lemon trees outside the glass doors.

Place these flower urns on top of the stone balustrade.

An armillary sphere is used for observing the stars and planets.

Straw sun hat

Dizzy the dalmatian
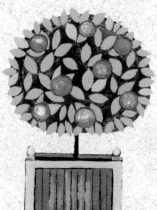

Place the table and chairs near the orange and lemon trees.

Orange tree

Orange

This silver tea set can go on the table.

A basket for collecting oranges and lemons

Orange tree

Naughty cat

Oranges

These flower pots can go on the steps next to the pergola.

PERGOLA GARDEN
(PAGES 14-15)

Stone well

Place this bird bath in the flowerbed.

This fox has wandered in from the park.

Large stone flower pot

Garden chair

Dovecote

Ornamental stone pineapple

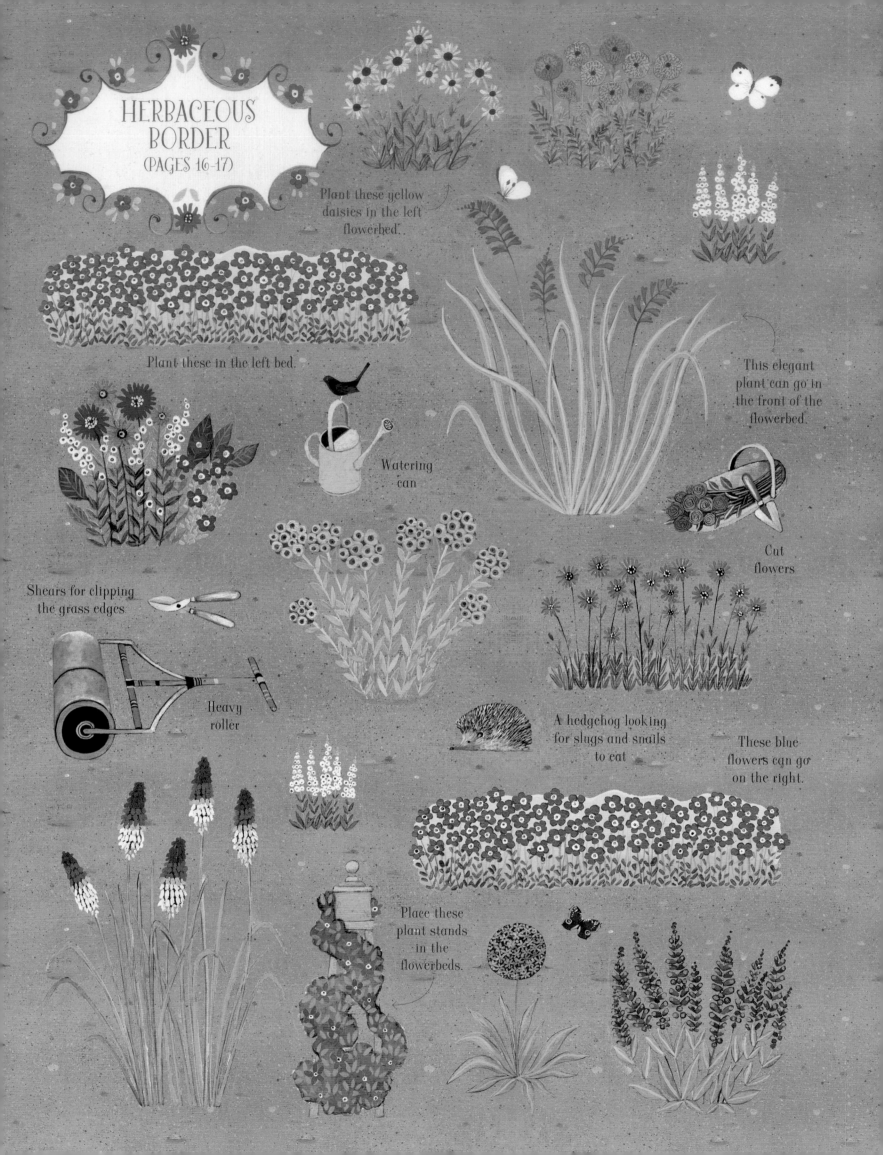

HERBACEOUS BORDER
(PAGES 16-17)

Plant these yellow daisies in the left flowerbed.

Plant these in the left bed.

Watering can

This elegant plant can go in the front of the flowerbed.

Cut flowers

Shears for clipping the grass edges

Heavy roller

A hedgehog looking for slugs and snails to eat

These blue flowers can go on the right.

Place these plant stands in the flowerbeds.

This purple flower can go at the front of the flowerbed.

Butterflies drink nectar from the flowers.

WALLED GARDEN
(PAGES 18-19)

Glass cloches

Watering can

Pottery cloches keep vegetables warm and help them to grow.

Place the beehives near the fruit trees on the back wall.

Wheelbarrow

Trowel

Chard is delicious steamed with some butter.

Place these rhubarb plants in the big bed.

The gardener has left this fork in a flowerbed.

GARDEN OF DISCOVERY
(PAGES 20-21)

These guard the Egyptian garden.

Sphinxes are mythical beasts, half human, half winged lion.

Place this bridge across the water in the Chinese garden.

Ornamental trees

Stone lantern in the Japanese gravel garden

Chinese garden building

Place this statue of a stork in the water next to the bridge.

Rock and gravel

Put this stone lantern in the gravel garden.

Stone and gravel

Stone model of a pagoda, a Chinese temple tower

This rake is used to make patterns in the gravel.

Water lilies

Place these stone lions against the hedge at the back of the Chinese garden.

Statue of Buddha

CONSERVATORY
(PAGES 22-23)

This exotic plant can go in one of the flowerbeds.

You can dot the pots and plants around the floor of the conservatory.

Place this large, bushy plant in one of the flowerbeds behind the bench.

All these plants like warm, steamy conditions.

This pot plant can go next to the bench.

Someone has left this book on the seat of the bench.

This small table can go next to the bench.

Place these plants in the front flowerbed.

Place this metal bench to the left of the conservatory doors.